D1275513

A NOTE TO PARENTS

Disney's First Readers Level 3 books were developed for children who have mastered many basic reading skills and are on the road to becoming competent and confident readers.

Disney's First Readers Level 3 books have more fully developed plots, introduce harder words, and use more complex sentence and paragraph structures than Level 2 books.

Reading is the single most important way a young person learns to enjoy reading. Give your child opportunities to read many different types of literature. Make books, magazines, and writing materials available to your child. Books that are of special interest to your child will motivate more reading and provide more enjoyment. Here are some additional tips to help you spend quality reading time with your child:

★ Promote thinking skills. Ask if your child liked the story or not and why. This is one of the best ways to learn if your child understood what he or she has read.

★ Continue to read aloud. No matter how old the child may be, or how proficient a reader, hearing a delightful story read aloud is still exciting and a very important part of becoming a more fluent reader.

★ Read together on a regular basis, and encourage your child to read to you often. Be a good teacher by being a good listener and audience!

★ Praise all reading efforts, no matter how small.

★ Try out the After-Reading Fun activities at the end of each book to enhance the skills your child has already learned.

Remember that early-reading experiences that you share with your child can help him or her to become a confident and successful reader later on!

— Patricia Koppman
Past President
International Reading Association

For Susan, Stuart, Caryn, and Evan
—J. K.

Paints and pencils by Sol Studios

First published by Disney Press, New York, New York.
This edition published by Scholastic Inc.,
90 Old Sherman Turnpike, Danbury, Connecticut 06816
by arrangement with Disney Licensed Publishing.

SCHOLASTIC and associated logos are trademarks of Scholastic Inc.

ISBN 0-7172-6460-2

Printed in the U.S.A.

TO SCHOOL— AND BEYOND!

by Judy Katschke
Illustrated by Sol Studios

Disney's First Readers — Level 3
A Story from Disney's *Toy Story*

SCHOLASTIC INC.

New York   Toronto   London   Auckland   Sydney
Mexico City   New Delhi   Hong Kong   Buenos Aires

"What's Andy doing?" Buzz asked. "He's zooming around like a shooting star."

"It's the 100th day of school," Woody explained. "He is bringing in 100 toys for show-and-tell."

Andy found his 98 army men. "I still need two more toys," Andy said.

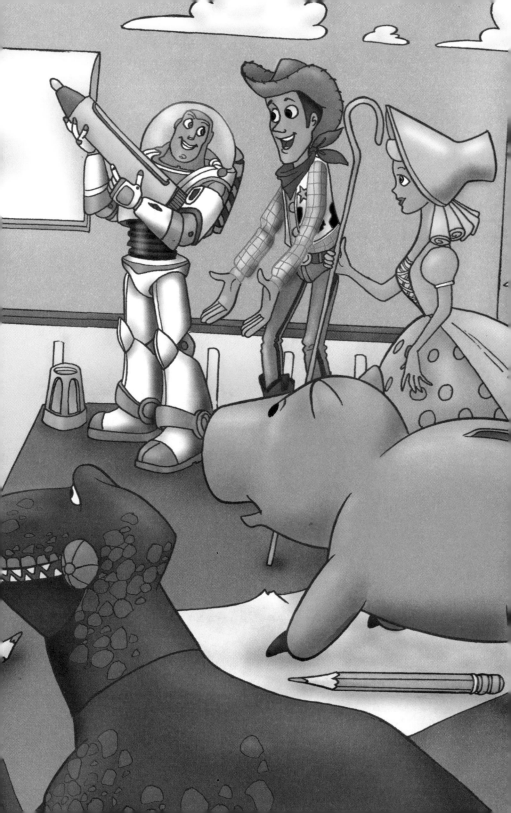

Andy picked Buzz and Woody.

"You have been chosen!" the alien said.

"It's too bad dinosaurs aren't allowed in school," Rex said. "I'd like to learn how to count."

"I can teach you how to count sheep," said Bo Peep.

"School sounds like a strange planet," Buzz said. "What if I don't like it there?"

"You will," Woody said. "There is lots of intelligent life in school!"

Sarge called his troops. "We're marching off to school, men! March! March!"

When Andy got to school, he put his
backpack in his cubby.
"See you later!" Andy told his toys.
He ran into his classroom.
Buzz and Woody peeked out of
the cubby.

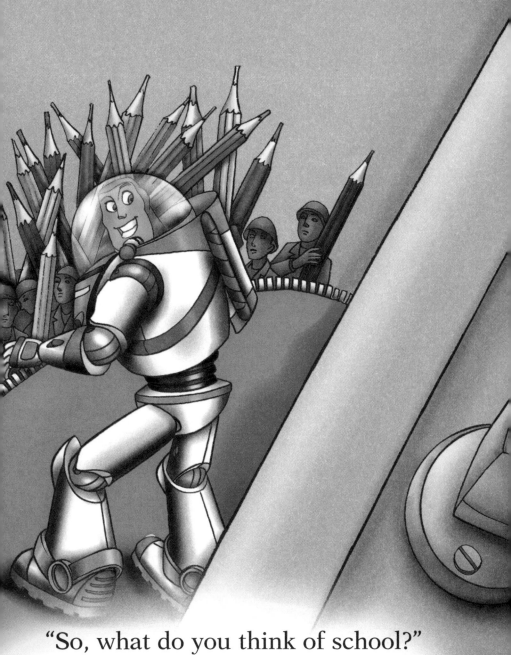

"So, what do you think of school?"
Woody asked.

Buzz hopped out of Andy's backpack
and looked around.

"I think I'm going to like it here!"
Buzz said.

Woody jumped out and ran to Buzz.
"Get back in that pack, Buzz!"
Woody said. "Andy needs us for
show-and-tell!"

But Buzz didn't listen.
"To Planet School—and beyond!"
Buzz shouted.
Buzz ran all the way down the hall.
Woody followed as fast as he could.
Buzz stopped in front of a classroom.

"Wait, Buzz," Woody warned.
"That's not Andy's class. It's—

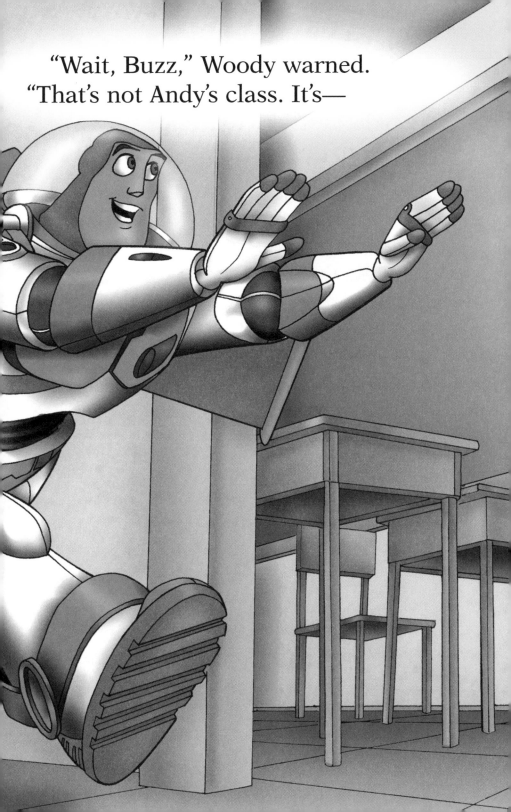

—KINDERGARTEN!" Woody was afraid. He saw finger-paints.
"Look! Toys!" cried a voice.
Woody froze. They had been spotted!

"I want the cowboy!" a girl screamed.
"I want the spaceman!" yelled a boy.

Back in the cubby, Sarge and his troops were worried.

"We've got to find Buzz and Woody!" he said. "Let's storm the mess hall!"

A woman stirred a big pot in the lunchroom.

"I love the smell of pea soup in the morning," Sarge sighed.

Suddenly, the woman saw
Sarge and his men.

"Green ants!" she screamed.
She grabbed a big can of bug spray
and pointed it at them.

"Code Red!" Sarge yelled. "Run
for cover!"

Woody and Buzz had escaped from kindergarten, but they got into more trouble.

"Look, Woody!" Buzz yelled, "It's a robot."

"BUZZZZZZZZZZ!" the robot called.

"This is one sharp robot," Buzz said. "He knows my name!"

Woody had to get Buzz back to
Andy's backpack before show-and-tell.
But Buzz ran off again.
"I hear beautiful space music,"
Buzz said.

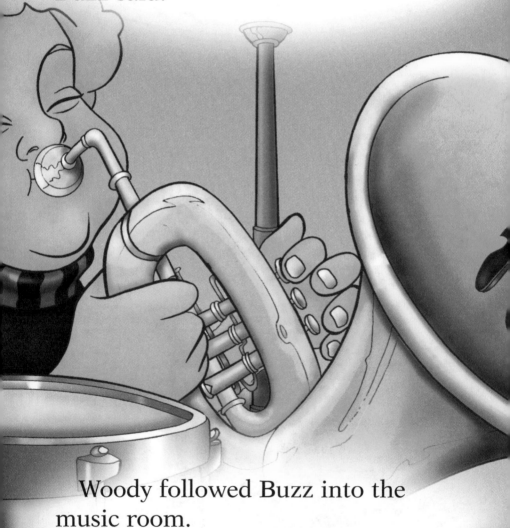

Woody followed Buzz into the
music room.
"This place is a blast!" Buzz yelled.

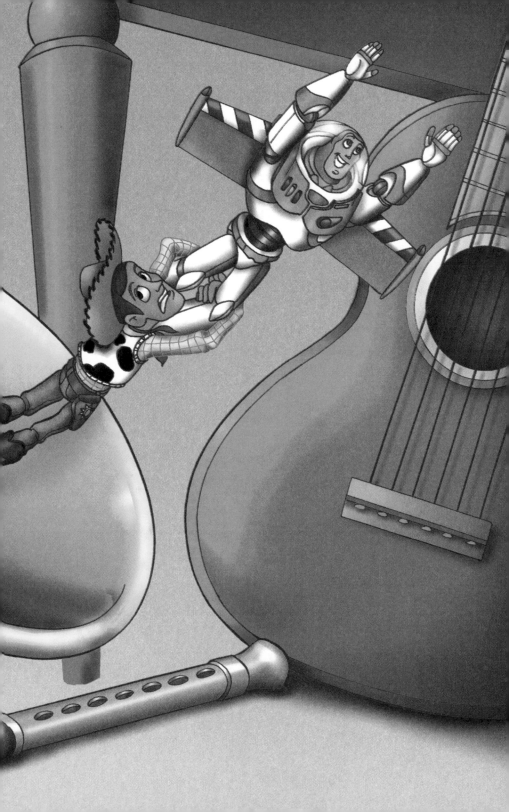

Meanwhile, things were getting sticky for the Green Army Men.
"Let's move!" Sarge shouted.
"We can't—SIR!" the soldiers yelled.
Sarge was worried. Finding Buzz and Woody was not easy!

Buzz and Woody crash-landed down the hallway.

Buzz cried, "We're in a crater!"

"It's a watering hole!" Woody shouted.

"Crater!"

"Watering hole!"

Woody turned a handle. A gush
of water knocked Buzz down.
"Hmm," Buzz said. "I suppose
you're right."

Woody chased Buzz into another room.
"We've found Star Command," Buzz
yelled. "This must be where they launch
their spaceships."

"Earth to Buzz," Woody said. "We
have to find Andy right away!"

But it was too late! Two bullies grabbed Buzz and Woody!

"These toys are mine!" yelled the first.

"They are *MINE*!" the second one yelled back.

Luckily for Buzz and Woody, a teacher stepped in.

"These toys belong to ME now!" she said.

Hmmmm, Buzz thought. She must be their leader.

Buzz and Woody were saved—
or were they?

The teacher tossed them into a dark hole. Buzz turned on his laser light. They were not alone.

"No toy has ever escaped Ms. Nelson's drawer!" a doll said.

"This place is making me jumpy," Woody said.

"We'll miss show-and-tell!" Woody said.
"Not true, Lawman!" came a voice.
It was Sarge! Sarge told his men
to open the drawer. The toys climbed
down to freedom.

They made it to Andy's backpack just in time.

"I brought 100 toys for show-and-tell," Andy said.

Buzz and Woody smiled.

100 Days of School

AFTER-READING FUN

Enhance the reading experience with follow-up questions to help your child develop reading comprehension and increase his/her awareness of words.

Approach this with a sense of play. Make a game of having your child answer the questions. You do not need to ask all the questions at one time. Let these questions be fun discussions rather than a test. If your child doesn't have instant recall, encourage him/her to look back into the book to "research" the answers. You'll be modeling what good readers do and, at the same time, forging a sharing bond with your child.

1. What special day is it at Andy's school?

2. Name all the rooms Buzz and Woody visited in Andy's school.

3. What was the thing that Buzz called a robot?

4. How many things can you name that you find in a school?

5. What words in the story have three syllables?

6. How many words can you make using the letters in "spaceman"?

Answers: 1. 100th day of school. 2. Andy's classroom, kindergarten classroom, lunchroom, music room, computer room. 3. an electric pencil sharpener. 4. *possible answers:* desk, chair, paints, colored pencils, pen, scissors, water fountain, computers, bulletin board, chalkboard. 5. *possible answers:* alien, dinosaurs, beautiful, another, watering, computers. 6. *possible answers:* ace, pace, pen, map, cap, cape, naps, name.